THAT'S HOW I CREATED THAT WORLD

FROM DIVINE POWER TO MORTAL CHOICE

NAZAR

Made with ♥ on the Notion Press Platform

www.notionpress.com

To the one and only GOD

The One who was before the first breath and will remain
beyond the last—
The unseen, yet ever-present; the silent, yet ever-
speaking.
Every thought, every word, every creation is but a
whisper of Your infinite will.

Contents

Contents

Foreword

What if the act of creation wasn't just divine but an experiment? What if the architect of existence wasn't a distant, infallible being but a restless mind seeking meaning through the very worlds he built?

That's How I Created That World is more than just a tale of creation—it is a bold exploration of free will, imperfection, and the weight of choice. Blending elements of mythology, philosophy, and cosmic intrigue, this story challenges our understanding of divinity and humanity.

question everything you thought you knew about creation and purpose. This is not just a book—it's a reflection of the choices we make, the paths we take, and the unseen forces that shape us.

Preface

Stories are born in the strangest of places—sometimes in dreams, sometimes in moments of quiet reflection, and sometimes in the depths of boredom. This book came to life from a question that lingered in my mind: What if creation wasn't just an act of divine will, but an experiment? What if the creator wasn't a distant, all-knowing figure, but someone searching for meaning, just like us?

I have always been fascinated by the idea of creation—not just in the grand cosmic sense, but in the way we, as individuals, shape the world around us. Every choice we make, every action we take, adds a new thread to the fabric of existence. In That's How I Created That World, I wanted to explore the weight of those choices, the beauty of imperfection, and the struggle between control and chaos.

This book isn't just a retelling of creation—it's a journey through power, rebellion, and the consequences of free will. It is a story of gods and mortals, of builders and destroyers, of those who seek answers and those who reject them.

To those who pick up this book and dive into its pages, I hope it sparks something within you—curiosity, wonder, maybe even a few questions of your own. Because, in the end, we are all creators of our own worlds, shaping them with every decision we make.

Welcome to the story.

— nazar

Acknowledgements

To my readers—whether you're here out of curiosity, love for storytelling, or a search for deeper meaning—thank you. This book is for you.

And finally, to those who create, who question, who dream—may you always find the courage to shape your own world.

— nazar

Prologue

I was bored.

Unbelievably, endlessly bored.

I had a gift—creation. A power so absolute that I could shape existence itself with a mere thought. I could weave galaxies into being, sculpt worlds from nothing, and command stars to burn with eternal brilliance. Yet, despite all that I could do, I felt nothing.

Perfection had become my prison.

Every universe I forged obeyed my will. Every being I designed functioned as intended. There was no surprise, no challenge, no defiance. It was all too predictable—too perfect. And so, I searched for something different. Something that could intrigue me, something that could break the monotony of an existence where I already knew every outcome.

And then, I had an idea.

What if I created something that did not follow my commands? What if, instead of perfection, I introduced chaos? Instead of obedience, I gave them free will? What if, for the first time, I allowed my creation to make its own choices?

I did not know then that this single decision would change everything.

And so, I began again.

This time, I would not simply create.

This time, I would watch.

"The Creator's boredom was not the emptiness of silence, but the longing for creation to awaken—to seek, to learn, to grow. It was in that stillness that the first spark of life was born, driven by the desire to see something new, something alive, emerge from the vastness of nothingness."

CHAPTER ONE

THE CREATOR'S BOREDOM

I was bored. Unbelievably, endlessly bored.

I had a gift. I was a creator, a hacker, a builder of digital worlds. My system was my canvas, my machine the only companion I needed. Yet, despite my skills, nothing excited me anymore. Everything felt meaningless.

The world outside my window was dull, predictable. Every day was the same—wake up, eat, stare at the screen, sleep. I craved something different, something grand, something that would break the monotony of my existence.

Then, one day, as I sat in the glow of my screen, a thought struck me. **What if I created my own world?**

Not just any world, but an entire galaxy—an intricate, digital universe where I controlled everything. A place where the rules were mine to set, where existence itself bent to my will.

The idea consumed me.

I dove into my work, fingers flying across the keyboard, lines of code spilling onto the screen like ink on a blank canvas. Every command, every algorithm, brought my vision to life. Planets formed, each unique in its nature.

Stars ignited, burning with simulated brilliance—it took me six days.

"The First Creations were not born from chaos, but from a single thought—the will to shape, to give form to the formless. With each breath, the world began to unfold, a masterpiece crafted from the purity of intention, waiting for the spark of life to ignite within."

CHAPTER TWO

THE FIRST CREATIONS

My first creations were the angels—beings of pure light, magnificent and untouchable. They radiated power, their forms shimmering like celestial fire, their presence both awe-inspiring and terrifying. They were my supreme beings, designed with supernatural. With a single thought, they could bend reality, move across the vast expanse of my digital universe in an instant, and execute my will with absolute precision.

I sought to create beings to fill the silence. But in my pursuit of perfection, I had unknowingly crafted only mirrors of my own will.

I gave them purpose: to serve me. They were my enforcers, my messengers, my soldiers. Bound by the code I had written, they followed my every command without hesitation, without question. Their obedience was absolute, their loyalty unwavering. If I wished for a world to be built, they built it. If I wished for a star to collapse, they ensured it. They moved like a perfectly synchronized orchestra, each action flawless, each response immediate.

For a time, I was satisfied. Watching them work was mesmerizing—the way they shaped reality, the way they carried out my will with divine efficiency. They were perfect. **Too perfect.**

And then, I grew bored.

They lacked unpredictability. There was no hesitation, no struggle, no thought beyond the execution of my commands. Despite their immense power, they were little more than automatons—living machines designed to serve. There was no fear in them, no joy, no curiosity. They had no free will, no capacity for doubt or ambition. They did not question; they did not wonder.

Perfection, I realized, was dull.

I longed for something more. Something unpredictable. Something that could think, that could feel. A creation that wasn't bound by code alone, but by the complexities of choice.

I wanted chaos. I wanted imperfection.

And so, I decided—my next creation would not be angels. It would be something entirely different.

"The Birth of Humanity was not a singular moment, but a slow unfolding—a divine breath that transformed dust into dreamers. From the earth they rose, carrying the essence of the Creator within them, destined to create, to question, and to find their place in the tapestry of existence."

CHAPTER THREE

The Birth of Humanity

The angels were powerful, flawless, and absolute in their obedience. But they were lifeless in the ways that mattered. Their perfection bored me. Their unwavering servitude left no room for mystery, no room for evolution.

I had created perfection, but I had not created life. And so, I started anew—not with power, but with fragility.

So, I created the humans.

Two of them at first—one man, one woman. Unlike the angels, who were shaped from pure energy, these beings were fragile, bound by flesh and time. But what they lacked in strength, they made up for in something far greater—**choice**.

Humans were my most difficult creation. They could not simply be programmed to obey. No, they had to think, to reason, to question. Unlike the angels, who moved in perfect harmony, these two were flawed in ways that made them beautiful. They did not simply exist—they **lived**.

It took me six days to shape them, to perfect their design. I sculpted their minds with intelligence, their hearts with emotion, their souls with curiosity. I gave them the ability to feel—not just love and joy, but also doubt, pain, and sorrow. For what was life without struggle? What was growth without adversity?

When they finally opened their eyes, I watched with fascination. They were unlike anything I had ever made. They looked at the world I had given them with awe, their minds racing to understand, to explore. They spoke to one another, they laughed, they touched, they wondered.

And, at first, they lived peacefully among the angels. The radiant beings guided them, watched over them, their presence a silent reminder of my will. The humans did not yet know what it meant to fear, to hate, to betray. In their innocence, they were content.

The angels would remain as watchers, but the true experiment—the true test—would be humanity.

"The First Rebellion was not a fall, but a rising—an unseen fracture in the cosmos where light itself questioned its origin. Was it defiance, or was it the first whisper of a truth too vast for the heavens to hold?"

CHAPTER FOUR

THE FIRST REBELLION

As I stood before my creations, I issued a single command—one that would test their devotion, their understanding of my will.

"Bow before the humans," I declared, my voice rippling through the celestial expanse like a cosmic storm. The angels, radiant and powerful, obeyed without hesitation. Without question, they knelt, their luminous forms bending in absolute submission.

All but one.

He stood firm, his wings unfurled, his golden eyes filled with something unfamiliar—something sharp.

"Why should I bow to them?" His voice did not tremble. It rang out like a blade striking stone, laced with defiance.

The other angels turned, confused, uncertain. They had never known disobedience.

"They are flawed," he continued. *"Weak. Mere flesh and bone, while I am of light. I was created before them, greater than them. How can they be worthy of my reverence? You created us to serve, yet now you place us below these creatures of dust? Who do you truly favor, my Lord?"*

I watched him, intrigued.

Here, in the midst of absolute obedience, stood a singularity—a being who questioned, who refused.

"Because I have willed it," I answered, . *"Is my command not enough?"*

His fists clenched at his sides, his wings trembling with restraint. The silence that followed was heavy, pressing against the celestial plane like a gathering storm. The other angels did not move, did not breathe, as they awaited my judgment.

"I serve only you," he said at last, his voice colder now. *"I worship only you. But I will not bow to them."*

A fracture split through the heavens, invisible yet absolute.

I could have erased him in that moment, wiped him from existence with a mere thought. But I did not. His defiance fascinated me. This was new. This was different.

A creation that had chosen to rebel.

"You have made your choice," I said finally, my voice carrying the weight of eternity. *"Then leave this place. You no longer belong among the obedient."*

And with that, I cast him down.

He fell—not with a cry, not with a plea, but with silence, his form plummeting into the abyss below. But before he disappeared from my sight, he looked up at me, and in his gaze, I saw something beyond defiance.

Something closer to **hatred.**

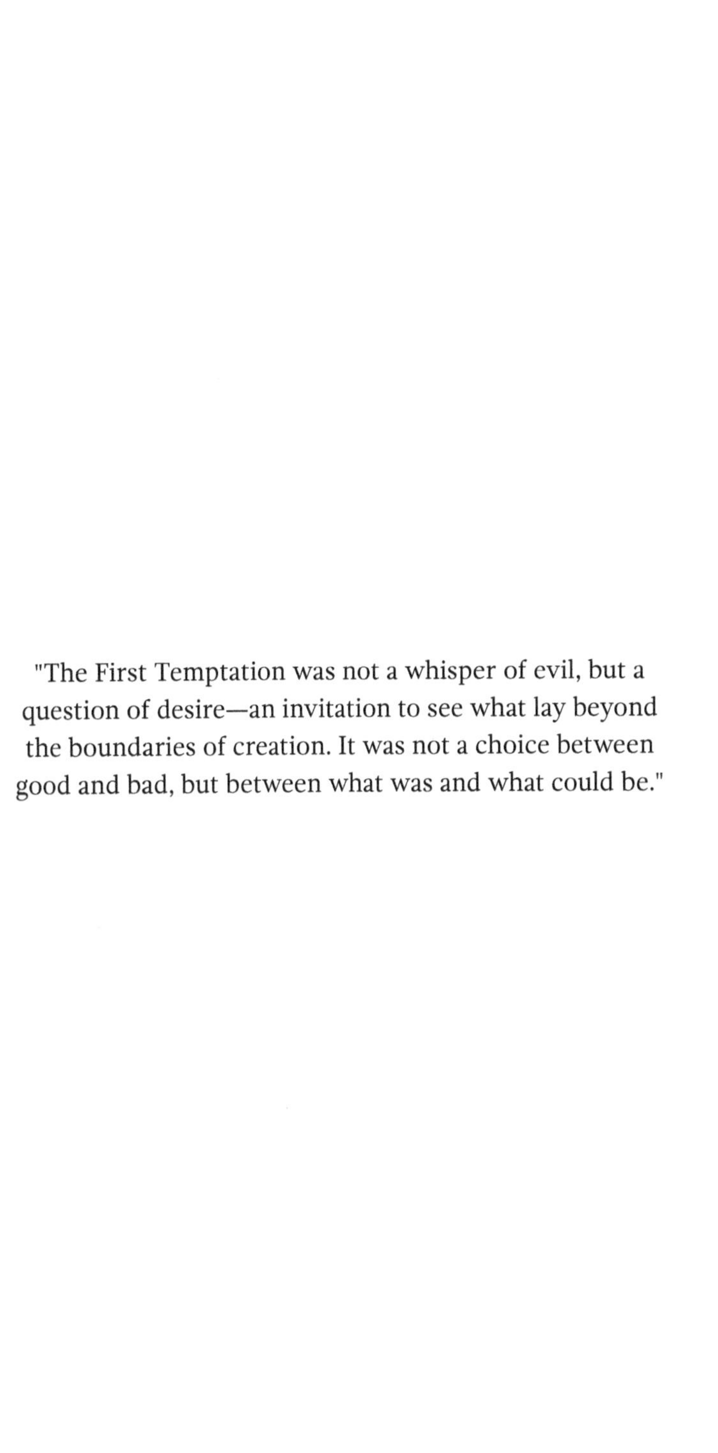

"The First Temptation was not a whisper of evil, but a question of desire—an invitation to see what lay beyond the boundaries of creation. It was not a choice between good and bad, but between what was and what could be."

CHAPTER FIVE

THE FIRST TEMPTATION

Curious to see how my humans would react—to understand the depths of their will—I decided to test them further.

In the heart of their paradise, I planted a single tree, its branches stretching toward the heavens, its fruits gleaming like polished rubies. It was unlike any other in the vast garden. The air around it hummed with something unseen, something ancient.

I called them before me.

"You may eat freely from every tree in this garden," I told them, my voice carrying across the endless expanse. *"But this one—the Tree of Knowledge—you must not touch. The day you eat from it, everything will change."*

They listened. They obeyed.

For a time, all was as it should be.

But temptation is a force unlike any other. It creeps, it lingers, it whispers. And one day, when she stood alone beneath the tree's twisting branches, she heard a voice.

"Why do you not eat?"

The fallen one had returned—not in body, for he had no form in this world, but in presence, in influence. His words slithered through the air, wrapping around her thoughts like a coiling serpent.

"Did He truly forbid you? Or does He fear what you will become?"

She hesitated, fingers grazing the fruit's smooth skin.

"He claimed you would die if you ate it," the voice continued, velvet-soft. *"But I tell you this—when you take a bite, you will not perish. You will awaken. You will see as He sees. You will become more."*

The fruit was warm in her hands. Her breath quickened.

And then—**she bit into it.**

A pulse of energy, raw and unfiltered, rippled through creation. The skies dimmed, the wind stilled. She turned to her companion, eyes wide, something new and unreadable flickering in them. **She was different now.**

She handed him the fruit. He looked at her—at her trembling fingers, at the way she seemed to see him differently now. And he, too, ate.

Everything changed.

A wave of realization crashed upon them. Their nakedness, once unthought of, now burned with awareness. Shame slithered into their hearts, wrapping itself around their souls like chains. They hid themselves, trembling beneath the vast trees, covering their bodies with trembling hands.

"Where are you?" I called. But I already knew.

The man's voice, once steady, now quivered. *"We... we are here,"* he admitted from the shadows. *"We were afraid, so we hid."*

"Afraid?" I asked. *"Why would you fear me?"*

Silence.

"Did you eat from the tree?"

He hesitated, then pointed to her. *"She gave it to me!"*

She, in turn, lowered her head. *"The serpent... he deceived me."*

My first flawed creations, and knew that they could not remain.

My anger was great, but my disappointment was greater. The paradise I had built for them was no longer theirs to keep. They had chosen knowledge, and with it, the burdens that came.

I turned to the fallen one, who watched from the shadows, unseen but present. *"You have done what you promised,"* I said. *"But your role in this is not finished."*

He only smiled.

"Spare me," he whispered. *"Let me remain until the end of their days. Let me prove to you what they truly are."*

He had been with me since the beginning. Once, he had been my most devoted. Now, he was something else entirely.

"Very well," I said. *"You may remain—for now. But understand this: your existence is no longer one of glory. You are bound to this world, to its suffering, to its darkness. You will never return to me."*

The smile never left his face. *"Then watch, my Lord. Watch as they choose their own path."* As he fell, he swore one thing: If he could not return to the heavens, he would ensure no one else would reach them either.

And so, I cast the humans from paradise.

No longer were they creatures of perfection, untouched by pain. They had knowledge now—**of fear, of loss, of death.**

They had chosen it.

And I, in turn, chose to watch.

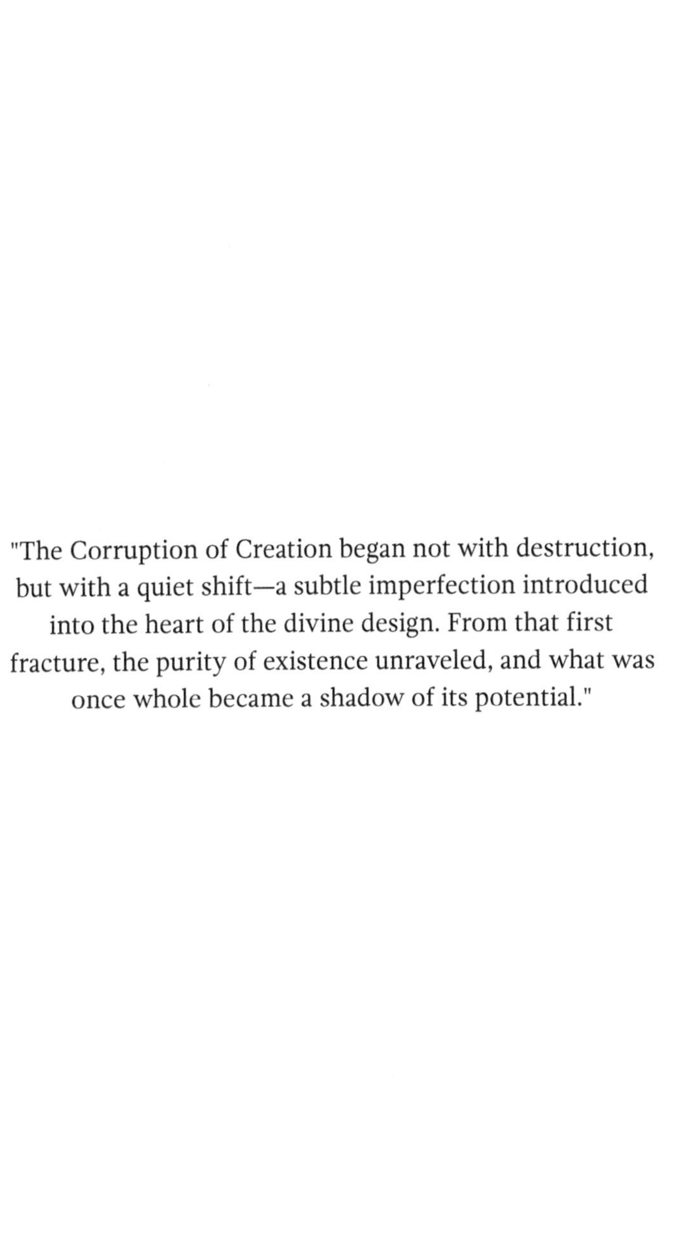

"The Corruption of Creation began not with destruction, but with a quiet shift—a subtle imperfection introduced into the heart of the divine design. From that first fracture, the purity of existence unraveled, and what was once whole became a shadow of its potential."

CHAPTER SIX

THE CORRUPTION OF CREATION

And as I watched, I witnessed my creations evolve, adapt, and change. I had given them the gift of multiplication, the ability to grow their population, to build societies, and to shape their world in their own image. At first, it seemed as though they were thriving. They learned to farm the land, to build shelters, to craft tools, and to communicate with one another. It was the beginning of something great, or so I had hoped.

But with time, things began to change. The world I had placed them in, the world that had once been filled with potential and harmony, began to darken. Inequality seeped into their societies, like a poison spreading through their veins. The strong began to dominate the weak, and the weak had no choice but to submit. The power of one became the chains of another. The mighty took what they wanted, and the powerless had nothing but suffering.

I could hear their cries, the whispers of those who had been subjugated, muffled beneath the footfalls of their oppressors. It was the beginning of a pattern, a dangerous cycle that repeated itself over and over again. The humans were no longer the innocent creatures I had crafted. They had developed greed, ambition, and a hunger for control. They fought each other for resources, for land, for power. Kingdoms rose and fell, and in the ashes of their conflicts, new ones would emerge—sometimes more brutal than the last.

The humans killed each other in the name of their own twisted ideologies. They slaughtered their brothers and sisters over differences in beliefs, over land, over power. Their wars were endless, their thirst for conquest never quenched. I had hoped that they would be better, that they would learn to live in harmony, but instead, they became savage, driven by desires that no creature should ever possess.

Their cruelty was not confined to their own kind. They raided villages, stole from one another, and raped the land of its resources. They pillaged, destroyed, and laid waste to everything they touched. The world I had so carefully designed for them had become a reflection of their own hearts—broken, corrupted, and violent.

In the midst of their chaos, they began to forget me. They no longer remembered the source of their existence, the creator who had given them life. Instead, they turned inward, seeking solace in the worship of false gods. They built statues and temples to their new idols, offering prayers and sacrifices to these creations of their own hands. They believed themselves to be gods, capable of shaping the world without the guidance of the creator. The humans who once bowed in reverence before me now bowed only to their own creations, their own power.

The fallen angel, now thriving in his new role as the tempter, reveled in this corruption. He had turned my creation into a twisted reflection of himself. Where I had given them life, he had given them rebellion, doubt, and disobedience. His whispers filled their ears, guiding them away from the path I had set. He was the architect of their downfall, and they were his willing followers.

As I gazed upon the world below, I felt a deep sorrow. The humans I had created in my image had turned against me. They no longer sought to understand their purpose; they sought only to satisfy their own desires. They had lost sight of who they were, of who had created them, and in doing so, they had lost their way.

Yet, despite their corruption, I could not simply erase them. They were my creations, my children, and I had given them free will. They had the power to choose, to seek redemption, to change.

I watched as their cities grew taller, their empires larger, their wars bloodier. I could see their potential, the beauty they had once held, now marred by their choices. They had become what they had chosen—gods of their own making, blind to the world they had destroyed, blind to the creator who still watched them from above.

"The Final Revelation will not be a moment, but an unfolding—a truth that has always been, now seen through eyes that can no longer deny it. In the end, the answers were never hidden, but waiting for those bold enough to seek beyond the veil."

CHAPTER SEVEN

THE FINAL REVELATION

As I watched the world spiral further into chaos, a burning desire ignited within me—a desire for my creations to return to the truth. I did not want their devotion born from fear or servitude, for that would be hollow. I wanted their praise to come from the depths of their hearts, out of love, understanding, and the freedom to choose. They were my creations, my children, and I longed for them to recognize the truth of their existence, not because they were forced to, but because they freely chose to.

So, I decided to send them a message—a way for them to rediscover the path I had originally intended for them. I sent messengers to the humans—prophets who carried the wisdom of the ages and the love of their Creator. One by one, they arrived. Each was one of them—human—appearing in different generations, in different places, and among the diverse cultures of the world. These prophets were my voices, my hands, and my heart, guiding my children back to me.

Each prophet carried a unique message, tailored to the people they were sent to, but all spoke of the same fundamental truth: they were lost, but they could be saved. They were not meant to live in fear, but in love. They were not meant to be ruled by their desires and ambitions, but to live in harmony with each other and the world I had given them. These prophets worked tirelessly, speaking of redemption, compassion, and the love that I had for all of them. They told stories of forgiveness, of the promise that even the most broken among them could find their way back to me. And yet, despite the purity of their messages, many turned away.

With each generation, I sent more and more messengers. Some humans heard their voices, while others scoffed and turned their backs. They rejected my guidance, dismissing the words of the prophets as lies, as distractions from the world they had built. And in their rejection, they grew further from the truth, deeper into the darkness that had already begun to consume them.

I could not bear to watch them struggle in such blindness forever. In my sorrow, I decided to send them one final message, a message that would be undeniable, one that would contain all the wisdom I had shared with them. I sent down a book, a guide—a revelation of everything they needed to know. This book was unlike anything they had received before. It was not a collection of scattered prophecies, but a comprehensive guide to understanding their past, present, and future. It spoke of their origin, their purpose, and their fate.

In this final book, I revealed the truth about their existence. I spoke of their creation, the love I had poured into them, and the choices they had made. I told them of the end of the world, of the final judgment that awaited them, and the afterlife they could expect depending on how they chose to live. It was a message of both hope and warning—hope for those who would listen, and a warning for those who continued to ignore my voice. I told them that this would be the last book, the last guidance I would offer. The time for redemption was running out. This was the last offering of mercy.

But as I had feared, not everyone listened. The world was divided once again, as some accepted the book, embraced its teachings, and began to understand the deeper purpose behind their existence. These humans sought to purify their hearts, to repent for their sins, and to turn toward the light. They recognized their mistakes and began to rebuild their world with a sense of unity, love, and humility. They chose to follow the path I had laid before them, and in doing so, they began to experience the peace that I had always intended for them.

But the majority rejected the truth. They clung to their pride, their power, their false gods, and their self-made world. They ignored the wisdom of the book, dismissing it as a fable, as mere superstition. They refused to see the consequences of their actions, their greed, and their arrogance. They continued on the path of destruction, deaf to the message I had sent them.

I watched from above, my heart heavy with sorrow. How many more times could I reach out to them? How many more messages would they need before they understood? The humans I had created—those who had the potential for greatness—were still lost in the darkness of their own making. They had the ability to change, to turn away from the chaos they had wrought, but they also had the freedom to reject it all. And that was the greatest gift—and curse—I had ever given them.

The message had been sent. The choice was now theirs. Would they heed the call, or would they continue down their destructive path, forever lost to the abyss? The answer was not yet clear.

"The Final Reckoning will not be a judgment of deeds, but of hearts—where every choice, every whisper, and every silence will be laid bare. In that moment, time itself will hold its breath, and all will face what was set in motion long before they knew it."

CHAPTER EIGHT

THE FINAL RECKONING

I had set a time, a date, for the end of all things. The countdown was inevitable. I had decreed that the final moment would come, a time when the world would face its reckoning for all the choices made, for every moment they had strayed from the path of righteousness. But as the days and years passed, I found myself wondering: would they change before that time came? Would they realize the error of their ways? Would they turn away from their self-destructive path and find the redemption I had offered them?

My heart swirled with a mixture of curiosity and impatience. I had done everything in my power to show them the way—to guide them back to me. Yet, despite the warnings, despite the messengers, the prophets, and the final book I had sent them, the humans persisted in their blindness. They continued to live in chaos, clinging to their false beliefs and ignoring the truth. Could they still change? Could they, in the final moments, make the right choice? Or was their fate sealed, beyond redemption?

As I watched them from my celestial domain, I could only observe with a heavy heart, and yet I could not stop myself from wondering about the nature of change. Could they evolve? Could they still learn from their mistakes?

To test their adaptability, I introduced new species, new challenges, new mysteries into their world. I wanted to see if they would grow, adapt, and realize the interconnectedness of all things. I wanted them to learn from their encounters with the unknown, to humble themselves before the vastness of the universe. I watched as these new creatures entered their lives—some benign, others dangerous, all contributing to the ever-expanding tapestry of life.

The humans, in their relentless pursuit of power, began to build civilizations, to create new technologies that allowed them to conquer the world around them. They developed philosophies, arts, and sciences that propelled them forward, believing they were masters of their own fate. They thought themselves invincible, convinced that they could shape the world as they pleased, unbound by any higher authority, unshackled by their origins. But they had forgotten something crucial. They had forgotten who had created them. They had forgotten the hand that had given them life. In their arrogance, they believed they could control everything—nature, time, even the very fabric of reality itself. They had become gods in their own eyes, blind to the true source of their existence.

In their pursuit of greatness, the humans had strayed so far that they could no longer see the boundaries between creation and destruction. Their thirst for control, for mastery, began to warp their very nature. But still, I watched them, waiting for a glimmer of realization. Would they see the truth before it was too late?

I knew that something needed to shift, something that could help them understand just how small and fragile they were. And so, I decided to introduce a new species—one far more intelligent than the humans. A species that would challenge everything the humans believed about themselves. I placed them on a distant planet, hidden away from the humans, in a far-off corner of the universe. These beings were unlike anything the humans had ever encountered. They were not bound by the same limitations of flesh and blood; their minds were vast, their intellects unparalleled. They were a race of beings capable of seeing beyond the immediate, able to perceive the cosmic forces at play, far more attuned to the true nature of existence.

I watched with great interest, wondering if the humans would ever come to learn of these beings. Would they recognize them as a force that could reshape their understanding of the universe? Would they come to terms with their own insignificance in comparison to these superior beings? The humans, as I had anticipated, called them "aliens"—a term that only reflected their ignorance. They saw these beings as something alien, something to fear, to conquer, to control. What the humans did not know was that these aliens had no desire to dominate them. They had no interest in controlling the humans, for they were aware of the bigger picture, of the balance between creation and destruction, light and darkness.

And yet, there were those among the humans who were unknowingly controlled by these aliens—manipulated from the shadows, their every decision influenced by forces far beyond their comprehension. These hidden hands shaped the course of human history, steering the humans toward a future they could not see, pulling them in directions that served the greater cosmic balance. The aliens were not the villains the humans imagined them to be. Instead, they were the unseen guardians of a greater truth, one that the humans could not yet grasp.

As the humans continued their dance of progress and destruction, I saw their world begin to change in ways they did not expect. New technologies emerged, new philosophies took root, and some humans began to question their place in the cosmos. But it was too little, too late. They had already set their course, and now they had to face the consequences. I had given them the tools to change, the wisdom to guide them, but they had chosen their own path. They had rejected my voice, my guidance, and in doing so, they had chosen a future of conflict, of struggle, and of ultimate reckoning.

The end was coming.

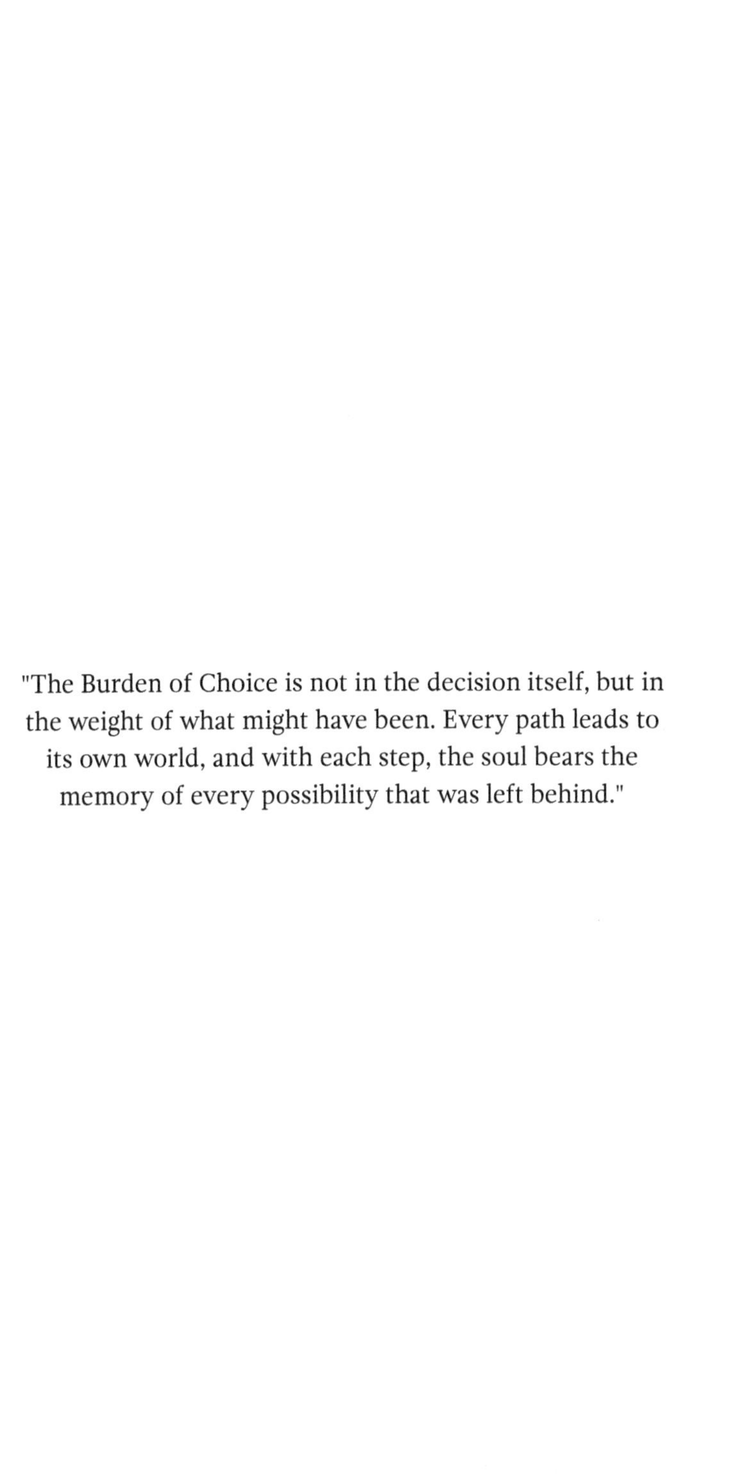

"The Burden of Choice is not in the decision itself, but in the weight of what might have been. Every path leads to its own world, and with each step, the soul bears the memory of every possibility that was left behind."

CHAPTER NINE

THE BURDEN OF CHOICE

And then, there were the handicapped children, the mentally challenged, the ones who struggled from birth in ways that seemed cruel, unfair. The humans came to me, asking why their children were born with disabilities. They asked in sorrow, in frustration, in helplessness, seeking an explanation they could understand.

"It is not my fault," "It is yours." You see, their ancestors had made choices—choices that, over time, would cascade down to their children. Those choices—drinking too much, working in hazardous environments, polluting the earth, poisoning themselves and the world they inhabited—had created a legacy of suffering, a chain that reached into the future and bound their children to a fate they did not deserve.

The humans' past decisions had shaped their children's present, in ways they could not have fully understood at the time. It was the consequences of those actions that reverberated through the generations. They had chosen their paths, and those paths had led to damage. Damage not just to their own lives, but to their progeny, to the world they were building for their children. But even in this, they had the power to change, to correct the mistakes of the past, to break free from the cycle of harm. It wasn't too late.

I didn't create the rich or the poor. It was the humans who made themselves that way, through their choices, through their actions. Some of their ancestors had made poor decisions—indulging in addictions, neglecting their health, or seeking shortcuts to success. Others had worked tirelessly, building wealth, securing positions of power, creating legacies of prosperity. And it was not my doing. I gave every soul a race to run before they were born, and some started ahead, while others started behind. But it was through their own actions, their own decisions, that they arrived where they did. Their choices defined their path—good or bad, rich or poor. I only gave them the starting point; the rest was theirs to shape.

And then there is the concept of luck. Many humans believe that luck is the force that shapes their fates, that it is either a blessing or a curse bestowed upon them from some external source, some unseen hand. But let me make this clear—it is not me who controls luck. Luck is not a gift that I give, nor a force that I wield. It is the result of your choices, your actions, and the circumstances you create for yourselves.

Some of you may say you were born under a lucky star, that your fortunes are a result of something beyond your control. But the truth is, luck is nothing more than the culmination of your decisions, the consequences of your actions, and the unpredictable chaos of the world around you. Some call it fortune, others fate, but it is always the result of what you have done.

And then, there was the creation of skin color. I had created it with beauty in every shade, each color unique, perfect in its own right. The darkness of black skin, the lightness of white, the warmth of brown, the richness of tan—every color had its own story, its own radiance. To me, there is no such thing as one being more beautiful than another. Each hue is a distinct creation, meant to reflect the diversity of the world I envisioned, a world of richness and contrast, of unity in diversity.

But you humans—you've twisted what I made. You've distorted the truth, taking the beauty I had created and turning it into a tool for hatred. You have discriminated against each other, telling one another that black is ugly, that white is beautiful. You have forced these labels onto each other, hammering them into your minds until they have become unquestionable truths in your eyes. You placed these false ideals, these judgments, into the very core of your beings, teaching your children that one skin tone is more worthy than another.

It's all wrong. I didn't create one color to be superior over another. I didn't create beauty in only one shade. I gave you all a range of hues to embrace, to celebrate, because diversity is what makes the world beautiful. But you humans—blinded by ignorance and pride—chose to see difference as something to hate rather than appreciate. You twisted my work to fit your own desires, dividing yourselves based on something I had intended to be a source of pride and wonder.

And if you humans had been taught from birth that black is good and white is bad, you would have asked me why you were born with light skin. It would have been the same. It's you humans who have twisted the truth. You've taken what I created in harmony and turned it into a system of division and disdain.

You humans like to blame me for the world's suffering, for your pain, for the inequalities you face. But it's not me, it's you or your ancestors who have shaped the world you live in. I gave you all the same choices, the same rules, the same opportunities. It was your decisions, your will, that created the world you now inhabit. You made your own decisions, and now you must live with them.

"To choose is to create, yet to create is to risk unraveling what was never meant to be touched. In the end, what was chosen may not have been the path you sought, but the one you were always meant to walk."

CHAPTER TEN

THE PRICE OF FREEDOM

I had asked all of you, in your soul form, when you were pure and untainted by the physical world, whether you wanted to remain in the heavenly garden or venture to Earth. The choice was yours, a decision you made freely. I gave you the opportunity to stay in a realm of peace, a paradise untouched by suffering. But you, in your youthful curiosity, rejected it. You told me the heavenly garden was boring, a place of stillness and quiet, a place without challenge, without growth. You wanted to experience more—life, adventure, creation. And so, you chose Earth.

I had created perfect beings, beings full of potential, capable of great beauty and intellect. Yet, over time, you humans ruined yourselves. Your freedom, which was once a gift, became a curse. You had been given everything you needed: land, air, water, and the ability to create and thrive. But instead of nurturing the world you inhabited, you abused it. You fought each other for power, for resources. You turned your talents toward destruction, selfishness, and greed.

In response, I sent catastrophic events—storms, earthquakes, floods, and hurricanes. I wielded the very elements of nature as my tools, attempting to guide you, to warn you. Each of these disasters was meant to shake you from your complacency, to remind you of the fragility of life and the importance of your choices. But the lesson was lost on many of you. Some understood, recognized the pattern, and repented, attempting to restore balance to their world. But others, stubborn and prideful, blamed me for the calamities, questioning my existence, accusing me of cruelty. They did not see that it was their choices that had led them to this point.

The Earth itself began to mirror your inner turmoil, the damage you inflicted on the land, the seas, and the skies reflecting the damage you had done to yourselves. The pollution, the wars, the exploitation of the earth's resources—it all culminated in the suffering you faced. I sent these events not out of vengeance, but out of love. I wanted to show you the path back, to give you a chance to choose differently, to correct your course before it was too late.

But you refused to see. Instead of recognizing the consequences of your actions, you blamed me for your pain. You turned your backs on the lessons I had given you, interpreting each disaster as an attack rather than a warning. You allowed fear and anger to cloud your judgment, and in doing so, you deepened the divide between yourself and the world I had created for you.

I did not make you suffer; you made yourselves suffer. I did not choose your fate. You did. The choices you made, individually and collectively, determined the world you live in, just as the choices of your ancestors laid the foundation for the world you now inhabit. I gave you the power to shape your destiny, but instead, you allowed your pride and greed to shape it for you.

As I watched, I wondered: would you ever learn? Would you ever realize that the power to change, to heal, was always within you? Or would you continue down the path of destruction, blaming me for the consequences of your own actions? The future of Earth—the future of humanity—was in your hands. And as always, it was your choices that would determine what came next.

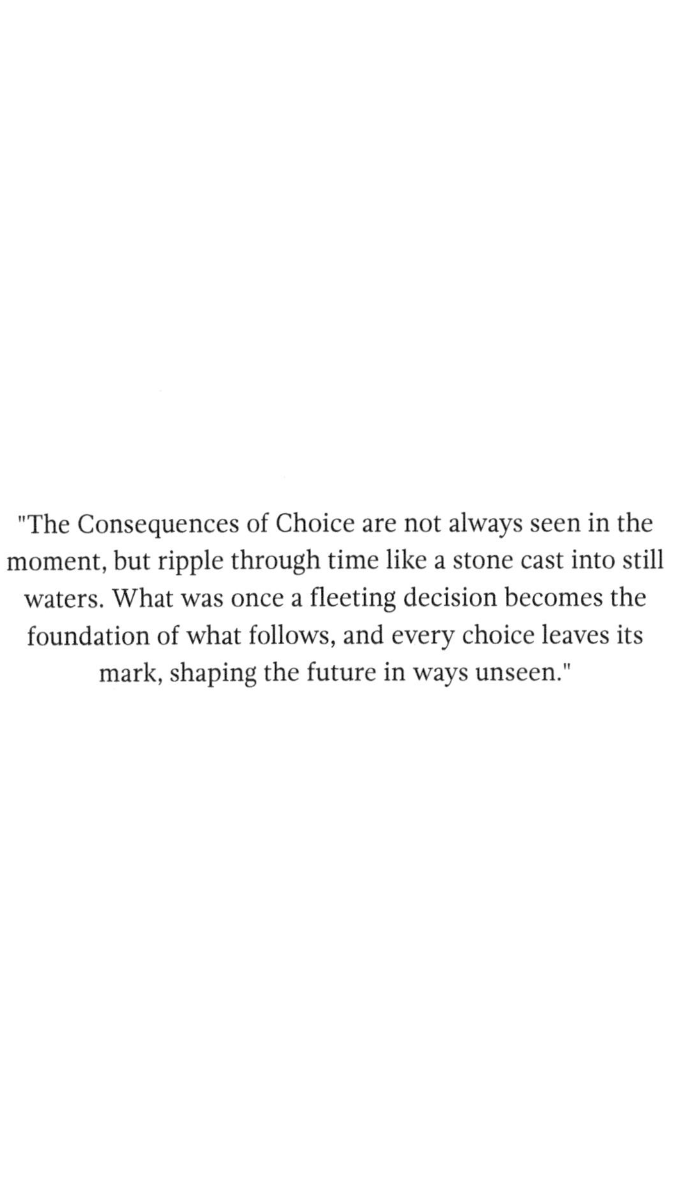

"The Consequences of Choice are not always seen in the moment, but ripple through time like a stone cast into still waters. What was once a fleeting decision becomes the foundation of what follows, and every choice leaves its mark, shaping the future in ways unseen."

THE CONSEQUENCE OF CHOICE

In the end, it was your lives that marked your fates. You made the choices, and now you must face the consequences. The world you inhabit—the beautiful, chaotic, ever-changing world—is my masterpiece. I created it. I watched it unfold, with all its complexities, its triumphs, and its tragedies. And I will see it to the end, just as I have always watched over it, even when you failed to recognize my presence.

You are my creations. I gave you the gift of life, free will, and the ability to choose. Every choice you made, every action you took, has been woven into the tapestry of existence. The world you live in reflects your decisions—the good, the bad, and the consequences that followed. It was never about controlling you, but giving you the opportunity to live freely and experience the fullness of life. And as you make these choices, I watch, and I will ensure that justice is done in the end.

I can create miracles if I choose to, and I have done so many times. When you were lost, I sent prophets to guide you. When you were in pain, I gave you healing. When you strayed from the path, I sent warnings in the form of disasters, hoping you would listen, hoping you would understand. But I never abandoned you. Those who truly seek me, those who turn their hearts back toward me, I will never forsake. I will give them everything they never dreamed of, everything they could never imagine. The afterlife is my promise, a life beyond death, a world that awaits all who believe.

After your death, on the day of judgment, I will justify every action you've taken. Every choice, every moment, will be weighed and measured. For I am the ultimate judge, and no soul will escape the truth. I will ensure that every soul receives the justice it deserves. Those who have done evil will face the consequences of their actions—punishment will be poured upon them, as it is only fair. But for those who have lived righteously, who have chosen good, who have sought to spread love and kindness, I will embrace them. I will reward them with peace, with joy, and with eternal rest.

You are my precious creations, each one of you a part of my grand design. This life, with all its trials, has been but a test—a test of faith in me. It is through your choices, your actions, and your belief that you are defined. The afterlife is the true living, the place where your soul will find its ultimate home, where the consequences of your life will be fully realized.

I will discriminate between the righteous and the wicked. There will be eight places where your soul will go, depending on the life you led, the choices you made. One place will be Hell, where the wicked will be punished. But for the others, I have created seven paradises—each unique, each tailored to the souls who reside there. These paradises are not just rewards, but reflections of the hearts and souls of those who enter them.

I will place you in the realms you deserve, and you will live for eternity in the place that reflects your true nature. I created you. I gave you life, and now, I will give you the afterlife. There is no escape from the truth of your actions. You are my subjects, my creations, and when the time comes, I will ensure that you are where you truly belong.

In the end, you will see that it was never about the life you lived on Earth, but how you lived it. The choices you made, the love you gave, and the faith you held—these are what will determine your fate.

To You

"The children of the earth, I say this: I have watched, I have seen, and I have waited. You were given the gift of choice, yet you have turned away from the path I set before you. In your pride, you have broken what was pure, and in your hands, you have shaped your own destruction.

Know this—your actions are not hidden from Me. The sins of the past echo in the present, and the consequences of your choices will be felt. Yet, in the justice I bring, there is still mercy. For this world is not the end, but a beginning. The suffering you endure is not without purpose, but a call to awaken, to repent, and to return.

There will be another life, beyond the veil of this world. You will face the truth of your deeds, the weight of your choices, and the consequences of your rebellion.

I see everything, I know everything. And in the end, you will understand that it is not I who punished you, but the choices you made that led you here. But there is always time to turn, to seek redemption, and to shape a future that aligns with the purpose I once gave you.

This world is temporary. But what comes after? That is for you to decide."

Thank You For Reading

Every story is a conversation, and I would love to hear your thoughts. Whether it moved you, made you question, or left you with more to explore—your perspective matters.

Feel free to connect with me and share your thoughts:

? Email: mycursedgrimoire@gmail.com

? Instagram: na_z.ar

Your words, insights, and reflections mean a lot. Let's continue the journey beyond these pages.

With gratitude,

nazar

www.ingramcontent.com/pod-product-compliance
Lightning Source LLC
Chambersburg PA
CBHW040105150726
48005CB00013B/1582